Published in the UK by

Don Bosco Publications

www.salesians.org.uk/bookshop

ISBN 978-1-909080-98-0

First edition 2023

Copyright © 2023 Anno Domini Publishing
www.ad-publishing.co.uk
Text copyright © 2023 Bethan James
Illustrations copyright © 2009 Honor Ayres

Publishing Director: Annette Reynolds
Design: Gerald Rogers
Pre-production: GingerPromo, Kev Holt

Printed and bound in China

Lots to Spot in Creation

Bethan James
and
Honor Ayres

sun   star   river   mountain

God made light and darkness,
day and night,
spring and summer,
autumn and winter.

winter
snow

wind

hills

6

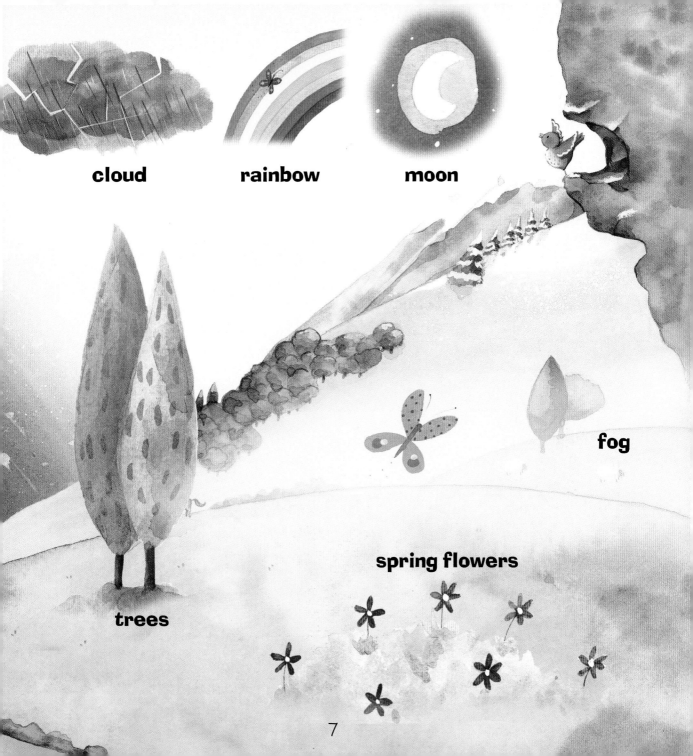

cloud

rainbow

moon

fog

spring flowers

trees

foxgloves   **toadstools**   **fruit tree**   **tulips**

God made pretty flowers and fruit and vegetables...

daisy

8

grapes and figs

palm

tomatoes

cypress trees

God made every kind of tree.

carrots

corn

9

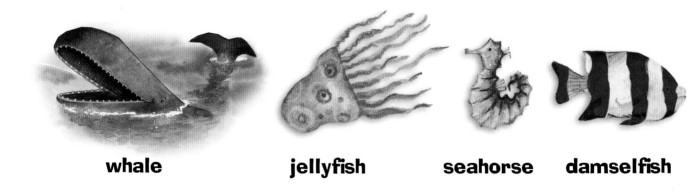

whale **jellyfish** **seahorse** **damselfish**

God made all sorts of creatures that live in the sea.

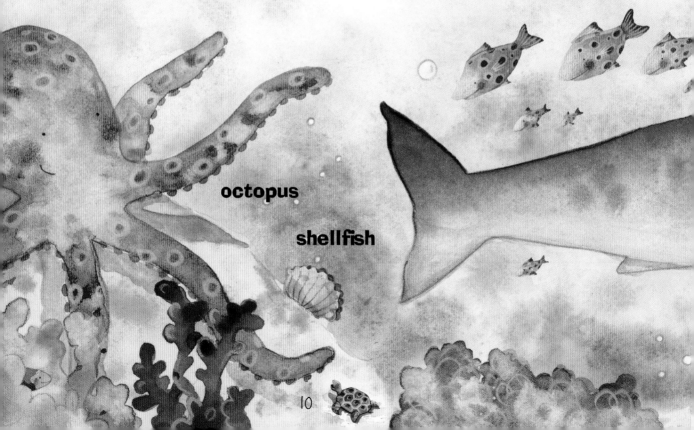

octopus

shellfish

dolphin

crab

penguin

turtle

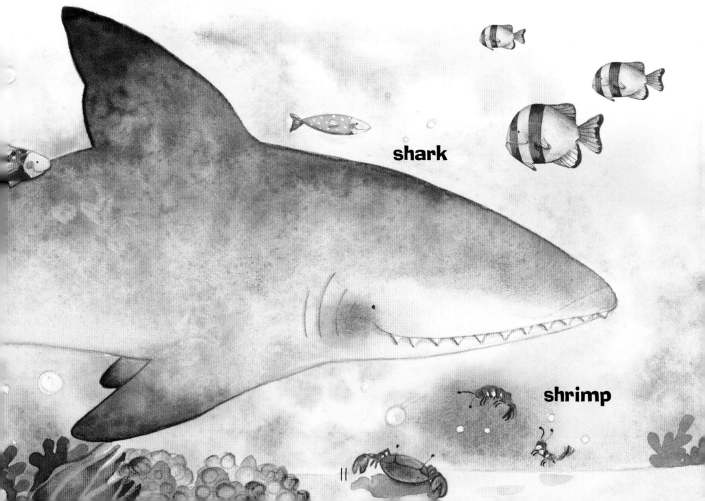

shark

shrimp

toucan

owl

dove

flamingo

parrot

robin

raven

ostrich

hummingbird

goose

God made all sorts
of creatures
with wings.

butterfly

sparrow

gull

13

spider caterpillar

ladybird dragonfly

God made
creepy crawlies
and creatures that
move without legs.

wasp

14

moth **locust** **bee** **snails**

slug

ant

15

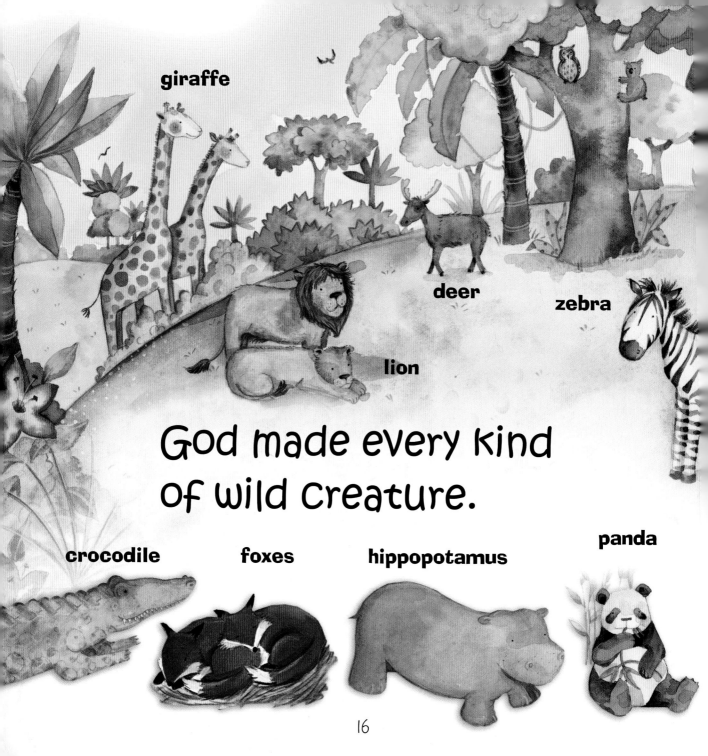

giraffe

deer

zebra

lion

God made every kind
of wild creature.

crocodile

foxes

hippopotamus

panda

elephant

peacock

koala

monkey

grey squirrel

porcupine

17

donkey **mouse** **dog** **goat** **chicken**

God made all the farmyard creatures.

cows

horse

mole

18

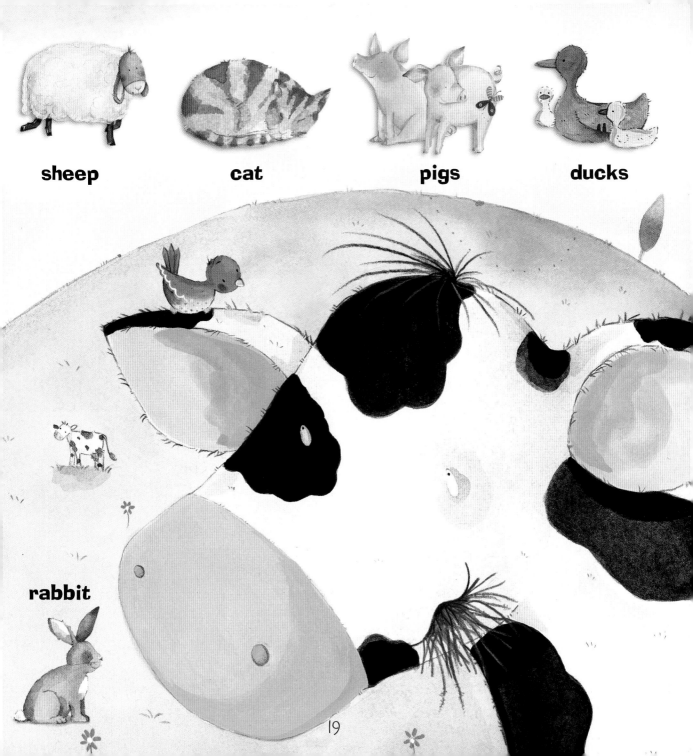

sheep

cat

pigs

ducks

rabbit

19

grannies

girls

God made
people of every shape
and colour.

20

babies

dads

mums

boys

friends

21

and God made

me!